October 2020

For the children of Eldorado—

MAY You Always enjoy books.

A Christmas Fable

For Emel, Rebecca, and Jacob
            — M. K.

For my neighbors and good friends in the woods
            —M. H.

A Christmas Fable

by Mark Karlins
illustrated by Maureen Hyde

Atheneum   1990   New York

When I was a young girl living in the mountains, and the days grew short and cold, I, like you, longed for Christmas. On a late-November morning I would wake to the odor of frost and notice, as if for the first time, how fully autumn had faded, leaving the trees bare, the plants in our garden brown, as fragile and hollow as ghosts. I would wait then. Oh, how I would wait! But late November moves slowly. December hardly moves at all. Through all the unending days, I wished, I dreamed, I waited.

"How much longer, Mama?" I'd ask.

"Oh, pretty soon," she would say.

Then I'd find my papa. "When's Christmas coming, Papa?"

"Soon enough," he would say, and smile a little. "Be patient."

Surely Christmas never did come soon, but it did always finally arrive.

n Christmas Eve our family packed
into the old blue pickup and drove to
Grandma's, where, as every year, all the folk
from the hollow gathered. Mama, who was an
herb woman and a midwife, carried a special
Christmas bread with rosemary and bay in it.
Papa placed a burlap sack of animal carvings
he'd made on the truck seat. I and my brothers
and sisters piled into the back, and, as Papa
drove, we gazed into the snowy woods, looking
for the robins and finches who, legend had it,
came back for a few brief hours on Christmas
Eve.

   Under the moonlight the snow on the fir trees
sparkled as though each tree was lit by a thou-
sand candles. And in the woods were shadow
upon shadow, some large, some small, here and
there one flickering, perhaps that of a robin or a
finch.

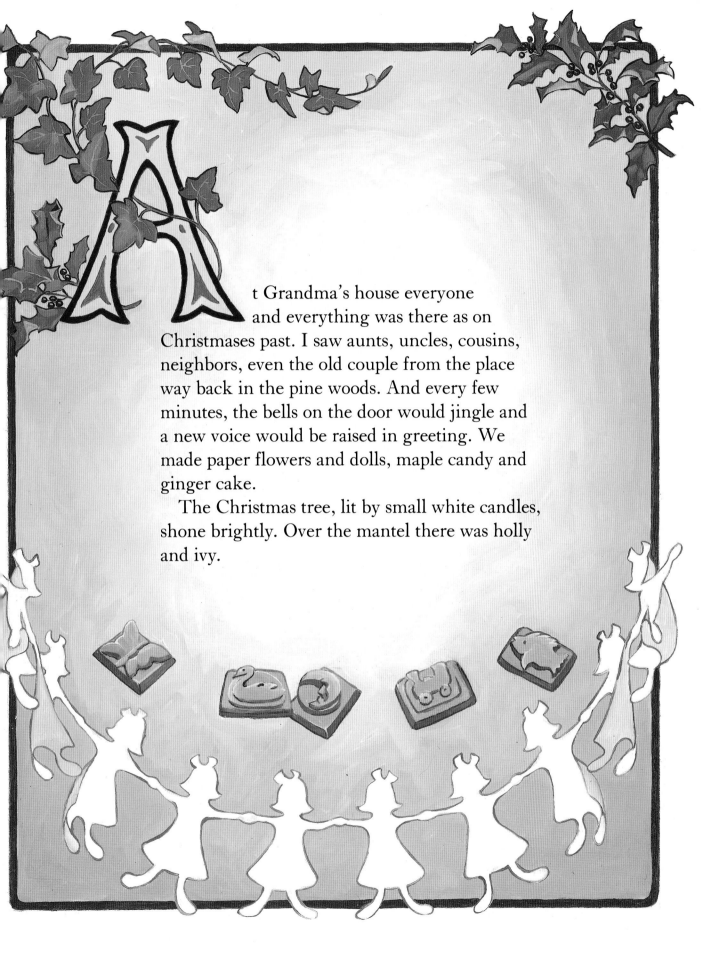

t Grandma's house everyone
and everything was there as on
Christmases past. I saw aunts, uncles, cousins,
neighbors, even the old couple from the place
way back in the pine woods. And every few
minutes, the bells on the door would jingle and
a new voice would be raised in greeting. We
made paper flowers and dolls, maple candy and
ginger cake.

The Christmas tree, lit by small white candles,
shone brightly. Over the mantel there was holly
and ivy.

And there was my favorite thing of all, the kissing bough. It looked like a little globe of the world. Hung on red cords and twined with boxberry and cedar, the round wire frame had inside it seven red apples on seven red ribbons. Around the globe were candles—so that the world was blazing with summer-bright light —and beneath it hung the mistletoe.

Aunt Rose pulled Uncle Jed under the kissing bough and gave his rough cheek a loud kiss. We all laughed.

Suddenly the door swung open wide and a cold wind blew through the room. The lights on the kissing bough flickered, almost going out.

In the doorway stood Old Grimble, who lived deep in the woods and was rarely seen by anyone. With his long beard and red wool shirt, he towered above us. His eyes flamed with anger. And his voice boomed, "You'll not have Christmas this year, I tell you. You shall not!"

In his arms was a wounded deer.

G rimble held the deer close, cradled against his huge body like a child. He walked into the center of the room.

"Do you not know," he said, "do you not remember that on this night the animals are blessed and speak? They must not be killed."

Grimble placed the deer before the fireplace and turned to leave.

"You'll have no Christmas, I tell you."

Then he left, but a chill stayed in the room, and it was dark and quiet.

Mama placed a blanket on the deer.

Papa carried it to the truck, and we went home.

That night Mama cared for the deer, washing and dressing the wound and placing a bowl of warm milk and honey before it.

But the deer did not drink, nor did it open its eyes.

"Go to bed now," Mama said, and we did, all of us children.

But we did not go to sleep easily, for we were thinking of what Grimble had said about Christmas, and we were thinking of the deer. As we lay in bed we could see the light from the living room, where Mama sat with the deer long into the night.

In the morning we saw that Grimble had been right. Christmas had not come. Not a single present lay beneath the tree. The tree itself seemed small and dry, the decorations limp and faded. Even the red holly berries over the mantel had lost their brightness, and some had fallen to the floor. The logs in the fireplace barely burned, giving off only a low blue flame. The room was chilled and icy.

I sat beneath the tree with my brothers and sisters, and we cried.

And so it was throughout our valley.

M ama continued to nurse the deer.
      She tried one remedy after another,
fixing poultices of foul-smelling herbs to dress
the wound or boiling other herbs, which heavily
scented the air.

   The deer neither woke nor ate. It only lay on
its side, barely breathing, its chest moving slowly
up and down.

   And during that time we, and everyone in our
valley, were so sad we barely ate. It seemed like
winter after a poor harvest, as though there were
no crops in the cellar, no jars in the pantry.

n the third dark morning we heard
a knock at the door. One of our
neighbors had come to see the deer. She knelt by
it, put down two bright apples, and said a few
words to my mother.

Then there was another knock and another
and another. By the end of the morning, all of
our neighbors had come to visit, and all had
brought gifts for the deer—a handful of oats,
some carrots, a few cubes of sugar.

nd by the afternoon there was
Grimble himself. He knelt down by
the deer, then, lifting it, cradled it again like a
child in his arms.

"You've done well," he said to Mama. "You
are a good herb woman, a good healer, for you
love well. And you others," he said, "you also
have done well."

Then, as Grimble held the deer and we all
looked at it, its breathing changed and the deer
opened its eyes.

Mama held up the bowl of milk and honey,
and the deer slowly began to lap it up.

o home now," said Grimble to the others. "You have done well. Perhaps," he said, his dark eyes beginning to sparkle, "perhaps..." But he did not finish his sentence.

Then Grimble himself left, and the sky, for the first time in three days, became bright with sunlight.

I woke early the next morning. The Christmas tree again looked bright and alive. The holly berries were red, the flames in the fireplace yellow and bright.

The deer herself rested beneath the tree. I went to her and knelt down. She turned her head toward me and sniffed gently.

Then I went to the window, and there, in the snow at the edge of the clearing, were other animals: raccoon, squirrel, fox, other deer, all perfectly still, looking off across the wide field toward the east hill, where now the red sun rose. How long, I wondered, had they been there, so close to my house? But before I could wonder for long, there, too, in the distance, I could see a man coming out of the hill's shadow, walking toward the animals through the deep snow. For a moment he paused, and across the field I thought I could hear him call to them, not just words but a brief song—or perhaps it was only the winter wind.

At the same moment I heard the deer stir. I turned and could see her ears pricked up, her eyes attentive. This was all for her! I am sure she knew, could sense the importance of this moment. She made a soft, breathy sound, almost a word, and then laid her head back down.

I looked back to the window just in time to see both the man and the animals turn back toward the woods and fade among the trees. The sun rose higher. I stood a moment longer and then I too turned, back to the warm room, the tree, and the deer.

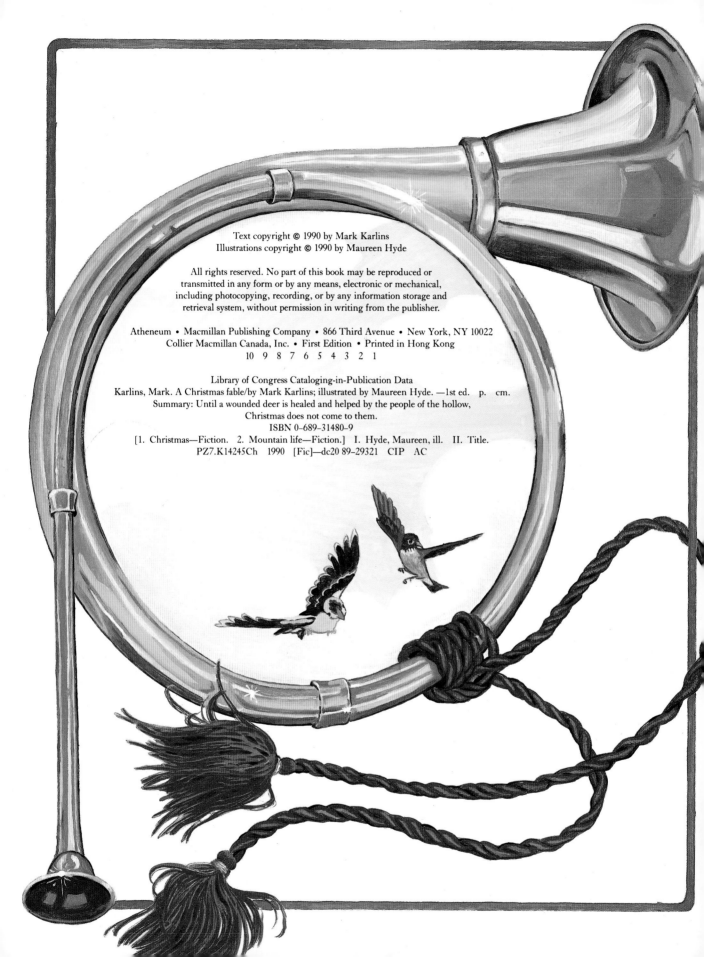

Atheneum • Macmillan Publishing Company • 866 Third Avenue • New York, NY 10022
Collier Macmillan Canada, Inc. • First Edition • Printed in Hong Kong
10 9 8 7 6 5 4 3 2 1

Library of Congress Cataloging-in-Publication Data
Karlins, Mark. A Christmas fable/by Mark Karlins; illustrated by Maureen Hyde. —1st ed.   p.   cm.
Summary: Until a wounded deer is healed and helped by the people of the hollow,
Christmas does not come to them.
ISBN 0-689-31480-9
[1. Christmas—Fiction. 2. Mountain life—Fiction.] I. Hyde, Maureen, ill. II. Title.
PZ7.K14245Ch 1990 [Fic]—dc20 89-29321 CIP AC